For Magda and Leonardo. —D. V.

For Clelia and Rebecca. —P. V.

Library of Congress Cataloging-in-Publication Data:

Names: Vogrig, Debora, author. | Valentinis, Pia, illustrator.
Title: Line and Scribble / by Debora Vogrig ; illustrated by Pia Valentinis.
Description: San Francisco : Chronicle Books, [2021] | Audience: Ages 3-5.
| Audience: Grades K-1. | Summary: Line goes straight on her way, while
Scribble wanders and zigzags, but they are still best friends, and can
work together with their individual perspectives to make art.
Identifiers: LCCN 2019058126 | ISBN 9781797201870 (hardcover)
Subjects: LCSH: Drawing—Juvenile fiction. | Perspective—Juvenile fiction.
| Best friends—Juvenile fiction. | CYAC: Drawing—Fiction. |
Perspective (Philosophy)—Fiction. | Difference (Psychology)—Fiction. |
Friendship—Fiction.
Classification: LCC PZ7.1.V66 Li 2020 | DDC [E]—dc23
LC record available at https://lccn.loc.gov/2019058126

Manufactured in China.

Design by Jennifer Tolo Pierce.
English translation by Debbie Bibo.
Typeset in Mark OT.
The illustrations in this book were rendered
with a crayon and fountain pen.

10 9 8 7 6 5 4 3 2 1

Chronicle Books LLC
680 Second Street
San Francisco, California 94107

Chronicle Books—we see things differently. Become part
of our community at www.chroniclekids.com.

Line
and
Scribble

By Debora Vogrig

Illustrated by Pia Valentinis

chronicle books · san francisco

This is Line.

And this is
Scribble.

Line goes straight on her way . . .

by plane

or by train.

Scribble wanders.

When Line digs a tunnel,

Scribble takes a ride on a roller coaster.

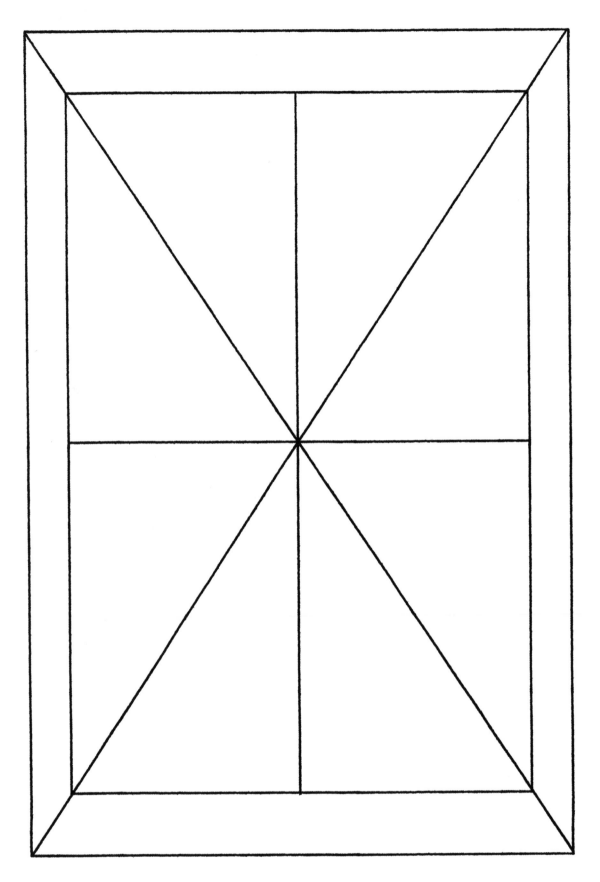

And if Line draws with a ruler,

Scribble scribbles, zigzags,
devises, dwells, and . . .

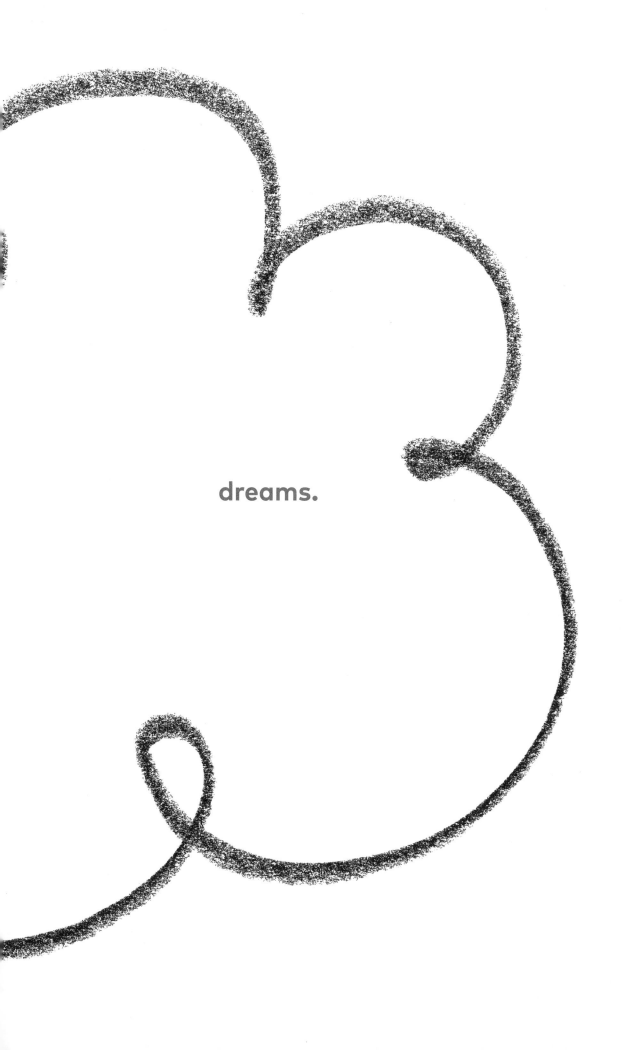

dreams.

Line says,
"Hey, Scribble!
Look at how straight my fur is!"

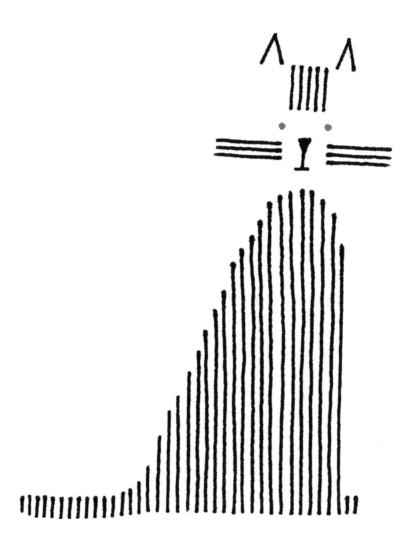

And Scribble replies,
"Hey, Line!
Look at how fluffy mine is!"

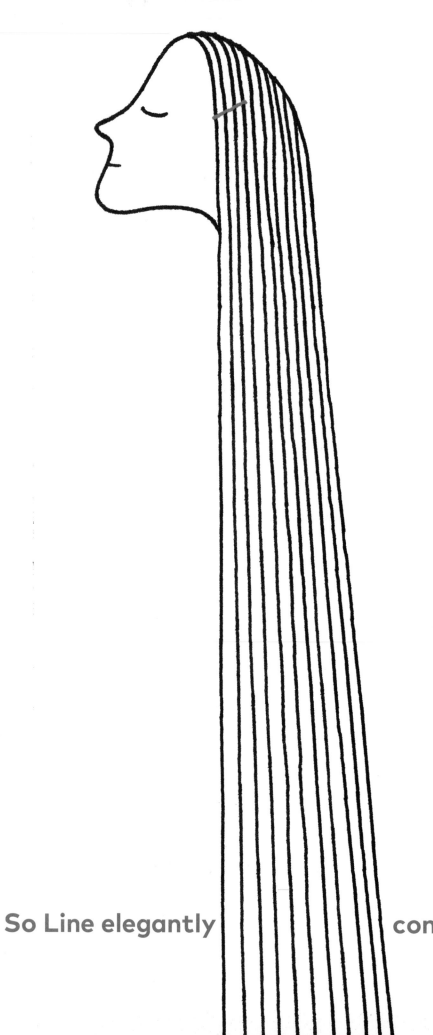

So Line elegantly combs her hair straight.

And Scribble curls hers with style.

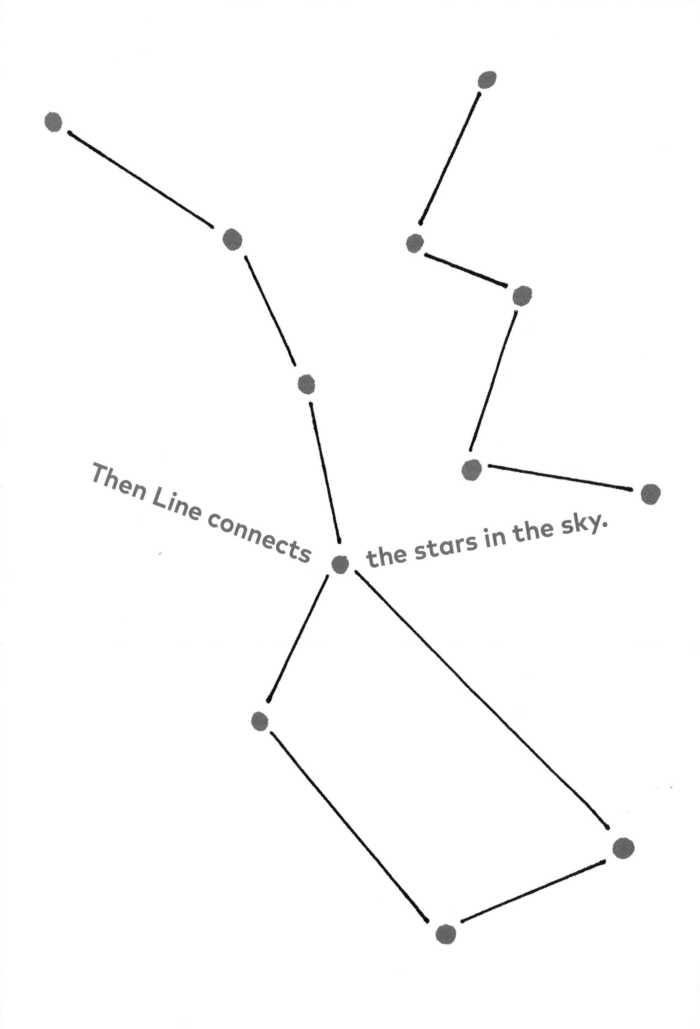

Then Line connects the stars in the sky.

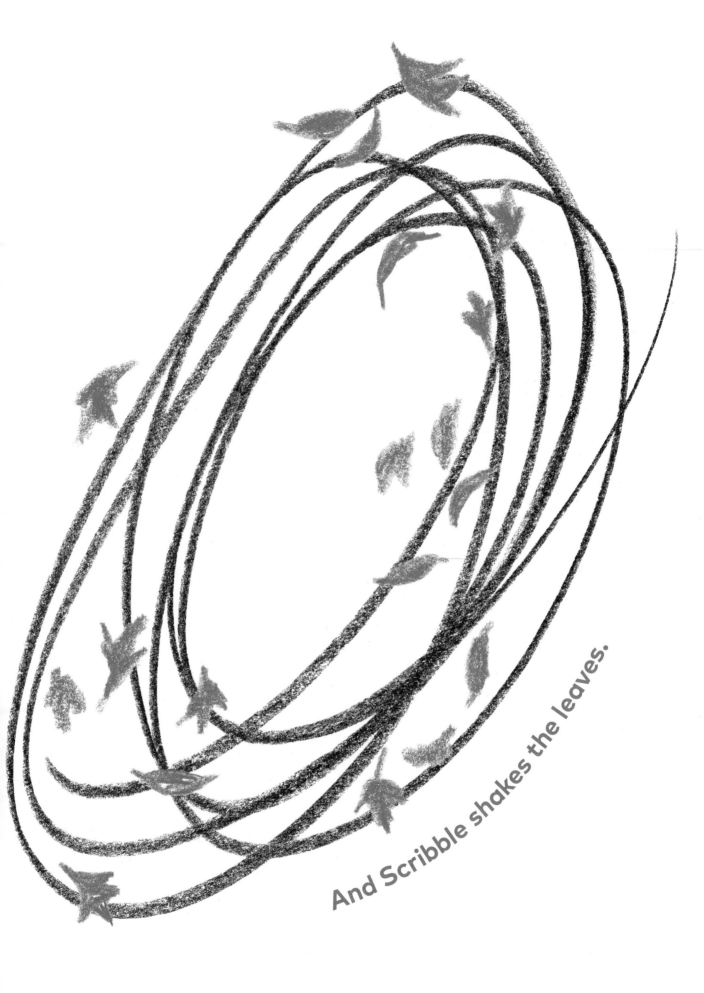

And Scribble shakes the leaves.

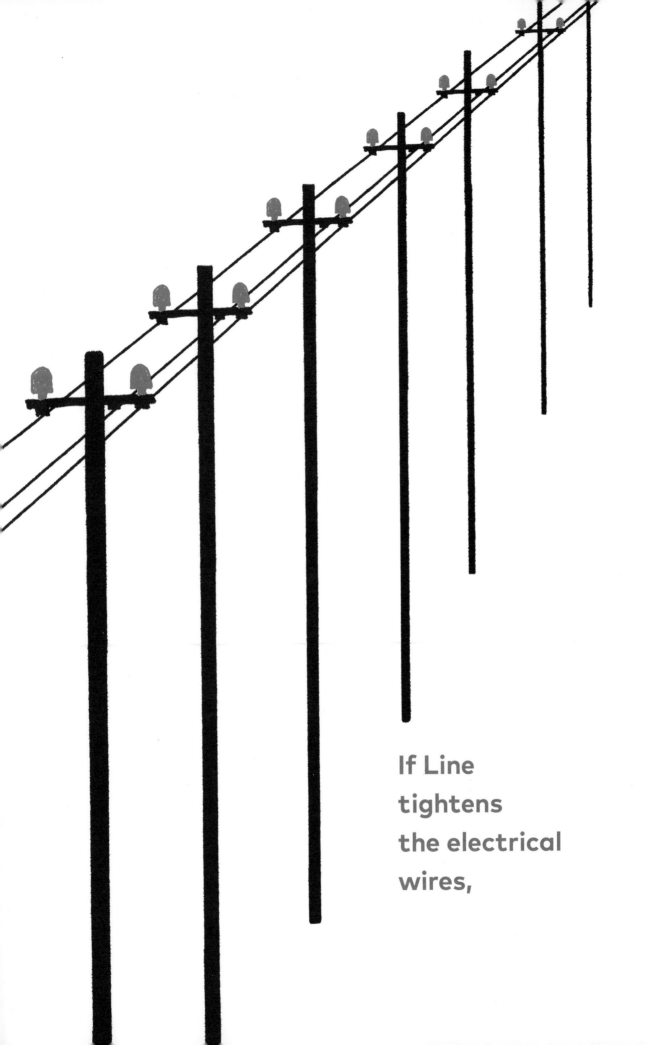

If Line
tightens
the electrical
wires,

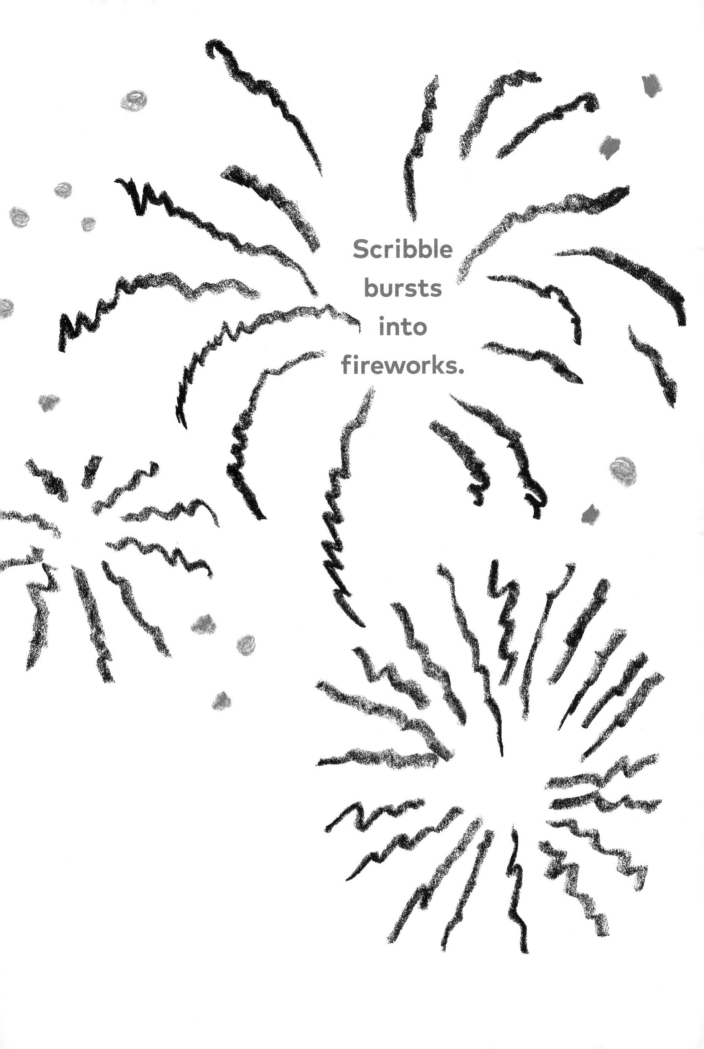

Scribble
bursts
into
fireworks.

So, Line walks a tightrope,

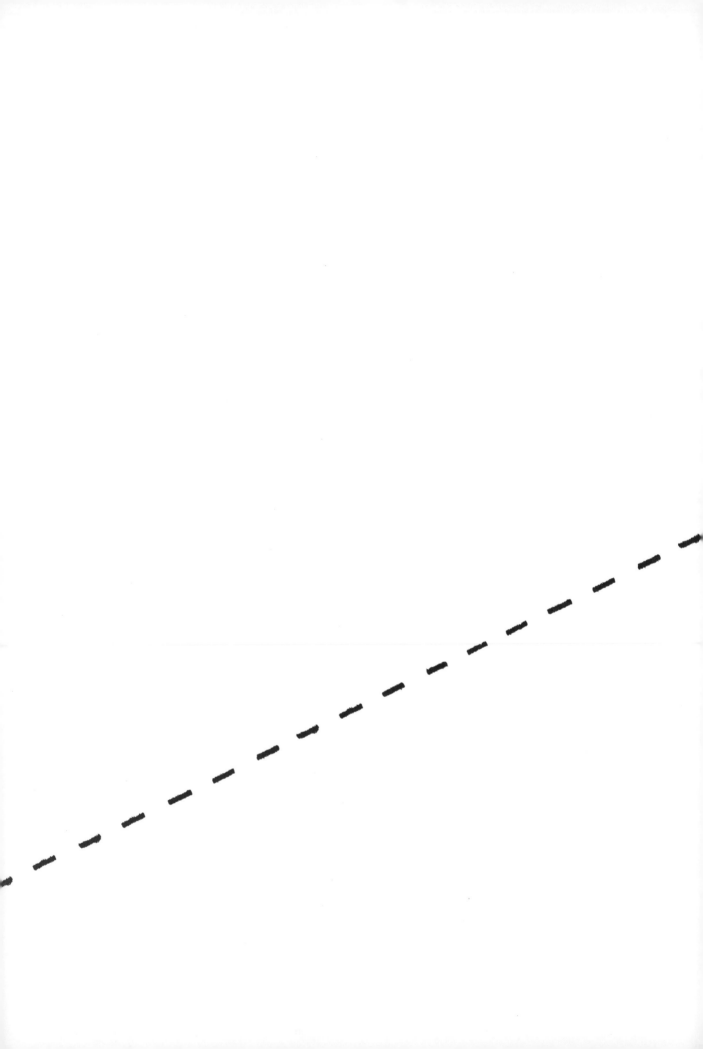

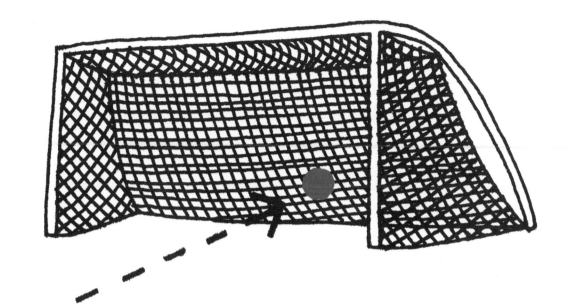

then yells,
"Look at that shot, Scribble!"

Scribble responds,
"Watch me dance!"

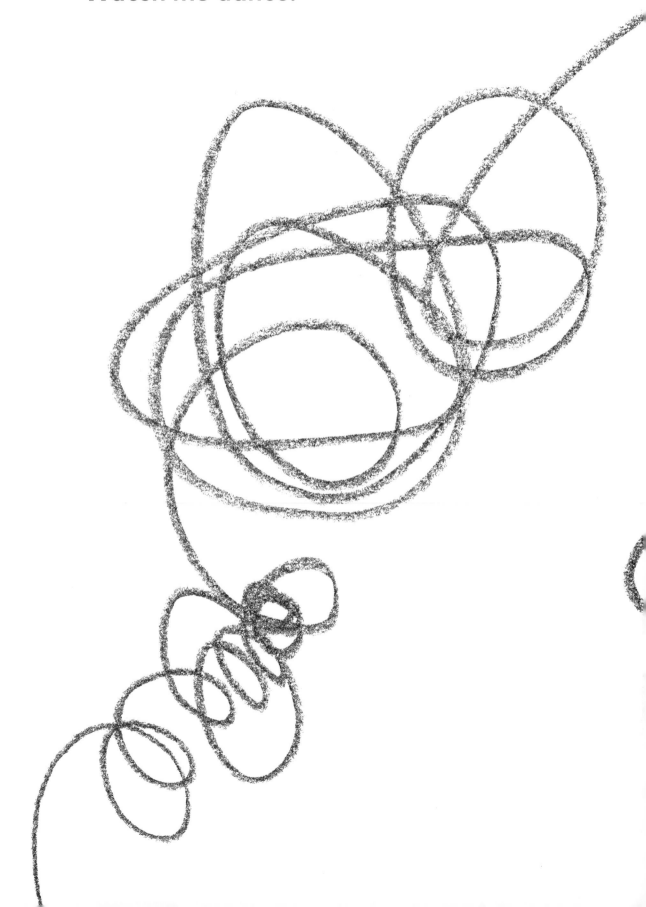

**And Scribble
twists, twirls, spins,
dances, jiggles,
and . . .**

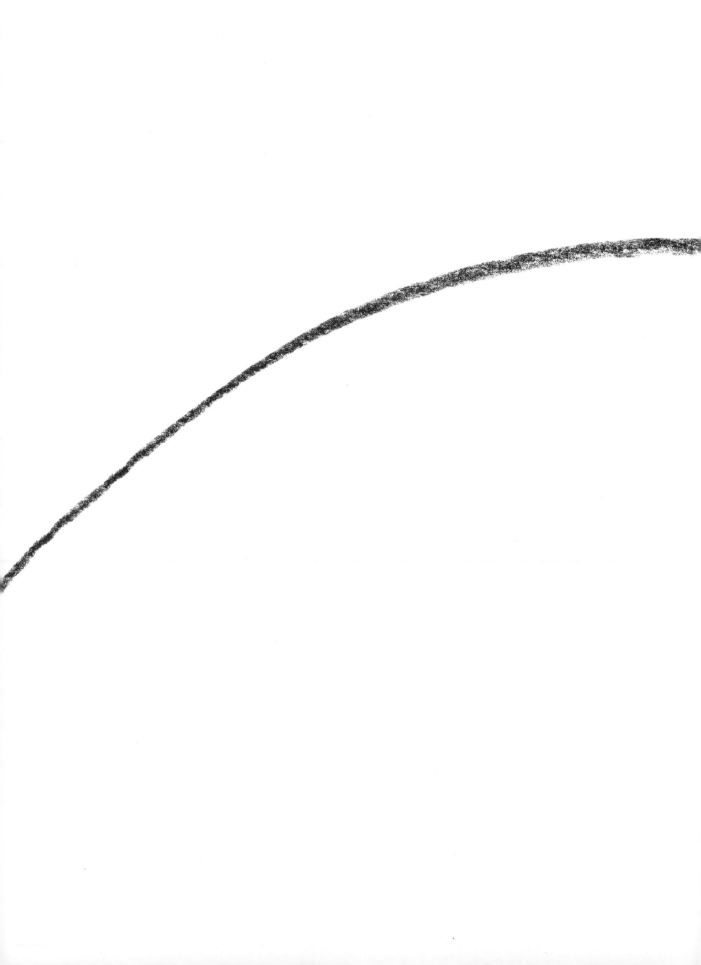

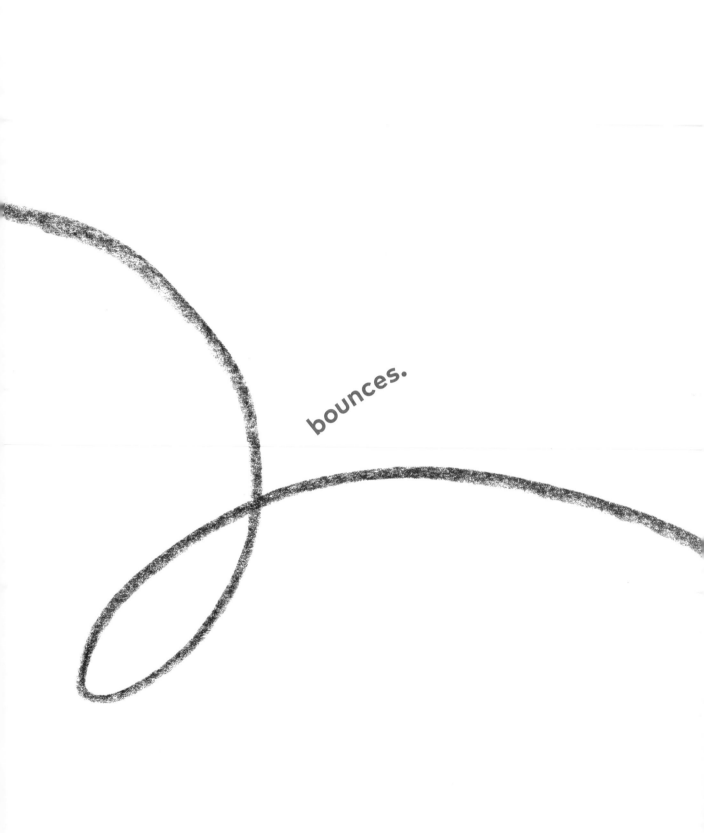

bounces.

Line asks,
"Do you want
a breadstick?"

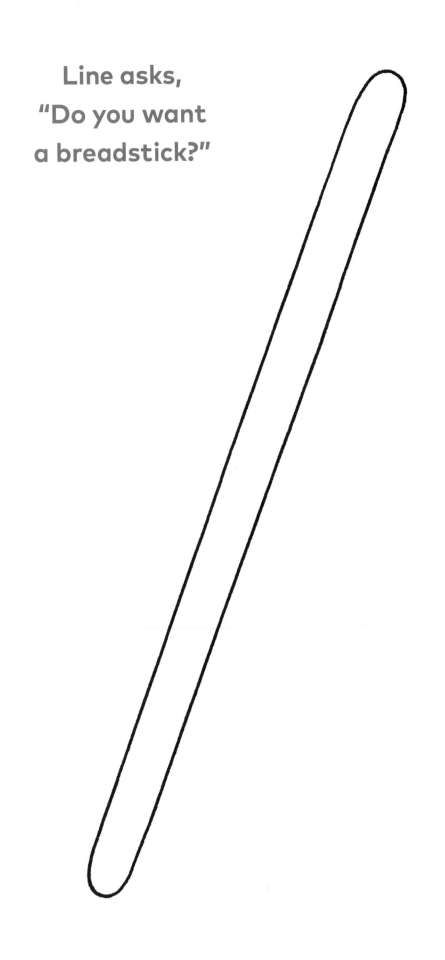

And Scribble replies,
"No, I want cotton candy!"

Line asks,
"Can you drink
with a straw?"

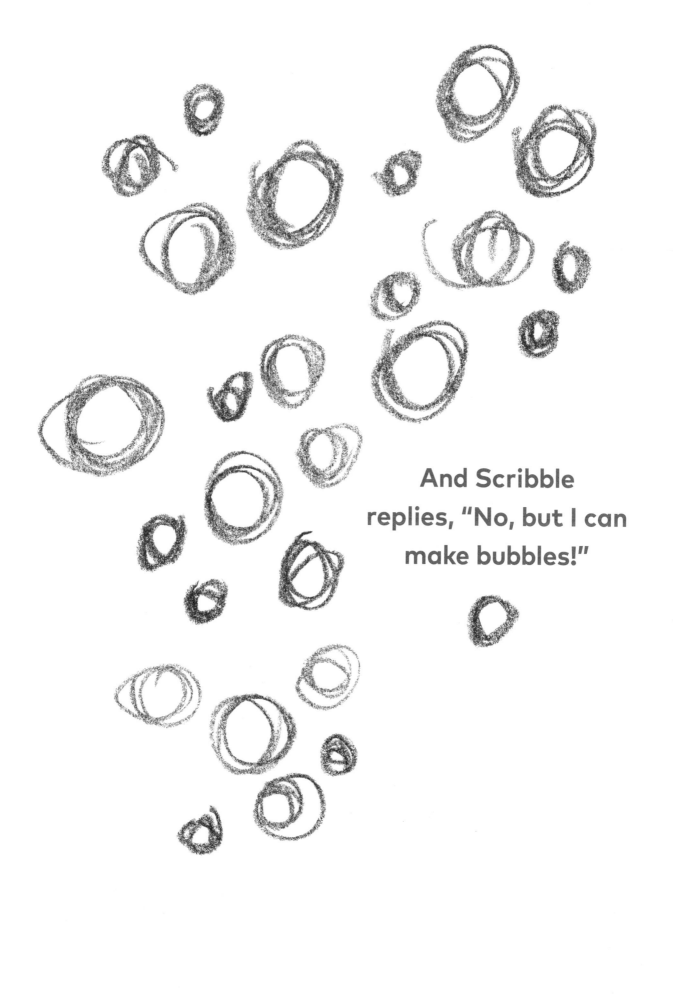

And Scribble replies, "No, but I can make bubbles!"

So, Line makes rain.

And Scribble
makes lightning.

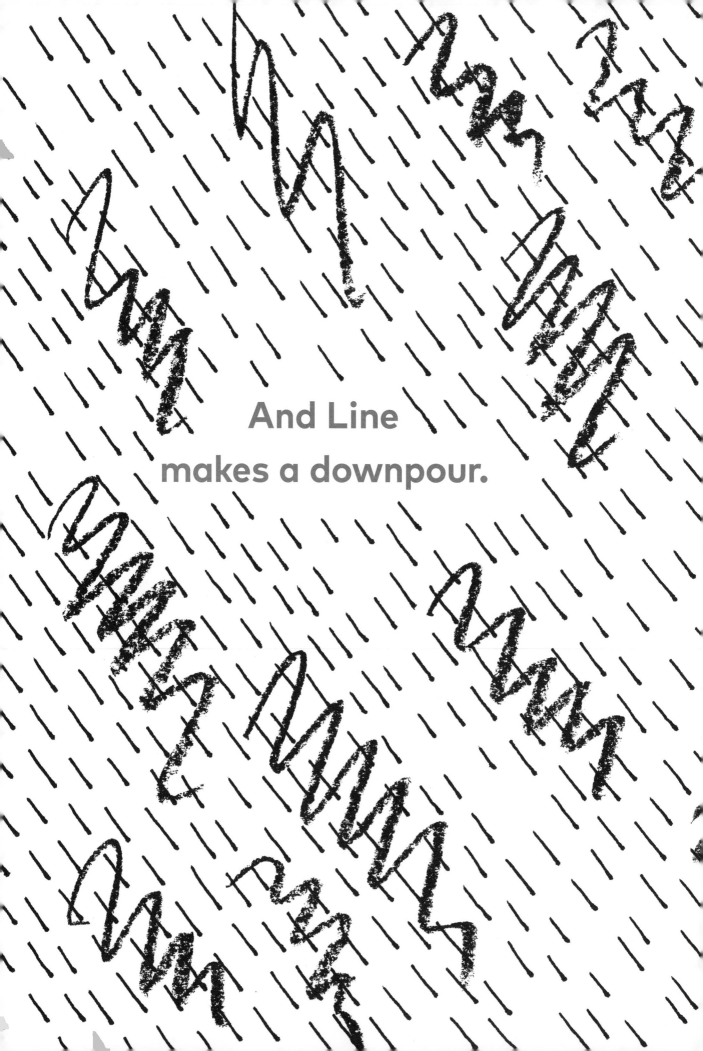

And Line
makes a downpour.

And Line makes the great flood.

So, Scribble makes

tornadoes,

gales,

cyclones,

and hurricanes.

What a

storm!

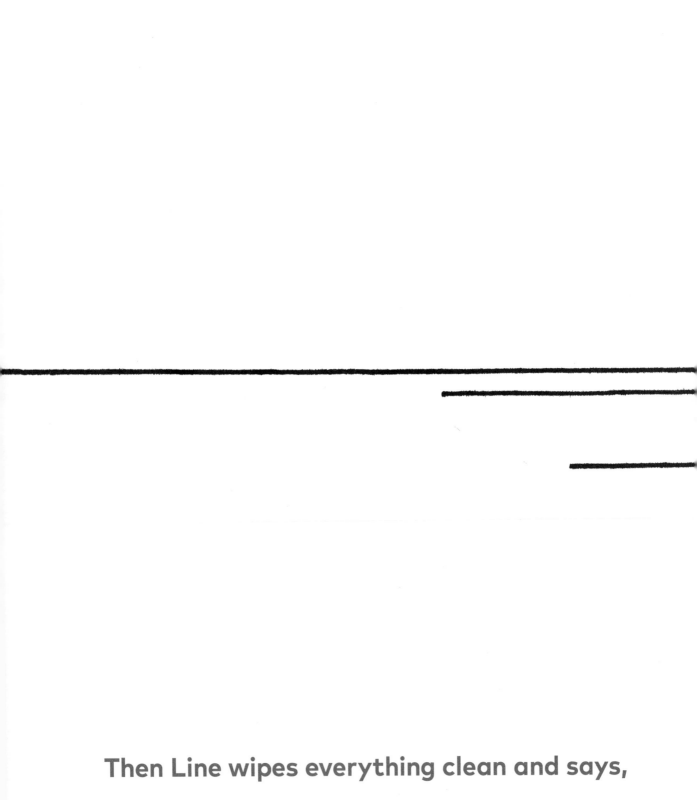

Then Line wipes everything clean and says,

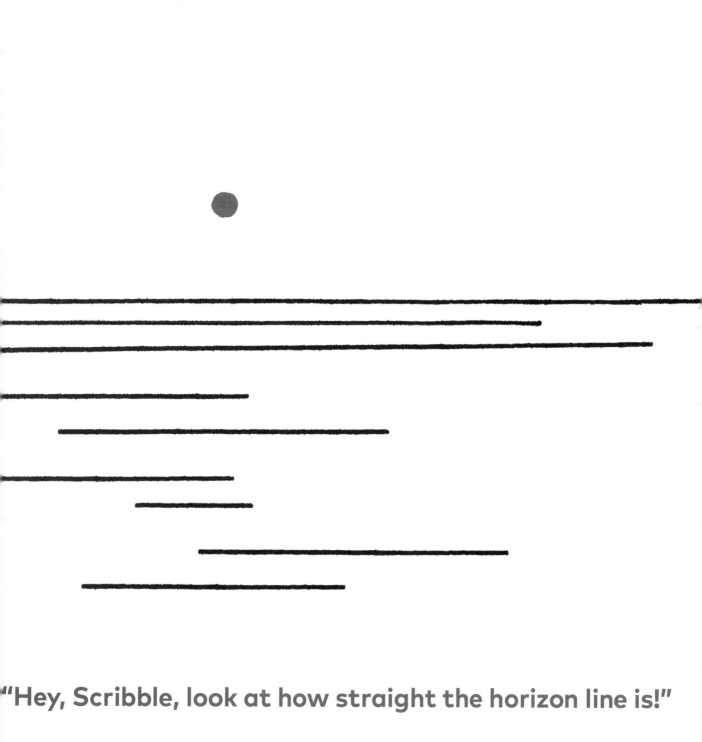

"Hey, Scribble, look at how straight the horizon line is!"

And Scribble replies,

"Well, *almost* straight!"